X-TREME FACTS: ENGINEERING

BUILDINGS

by Catherine C. Finan

Minneapolis, Minnesota

Credits:
Cover and title page, opasso/Shutterstock.com; 4 top, Richard Cavalleri/Shutterstock; 4 top left, Gorodenkoff/Shutterstock; 4 top right, cristovao/Shutterstock; 4 bottom, Bernard Gagnon/Creative Commons; 5 top left, Michael Warwick/Shutterstock.com; 5 top right, muratart/Shutterstock; 5 top far right, Albert Kretschmer and Dr. Carl Rohrbach/Public Domain; 5 bottom, Epel/Shutterstock.com; 5 bottom left, Jat306/Shutterstock; 5 bottom right, Wiper México/Creative Commons; 6 top, Djehouty/Creative Commons; 6 bottom, Acdixon/Creative Commons; 7 top left, Victoria Kurylo/Shutterstock; 7 top right, Wangkun Jia/Shutterstock; 7 top middle left, LightField Studios/Shutterstock; 7 top middle right, Lopolo/Shutterstock; 7 middle, Windmemories/Creative Commons; 7 bottom, Utente:FeaturedPics/Creative Commons; 7 bottom left, Juan Antonio de Ribera/Public Domain; 7 bottom right, Nicolao Landucci/Public Domain; 8 bottom, Tony Hisgett/Creative Commons; 8 bottom left, vadimmmus/Shutterstock; 9 top, javarman/Shutterstock; 9 top left, Mauro Rodrigues/Shutterstock; 9 top right, Dmitry Chulov/Shutterstock.com; 9 middle, Ken & Nyetta/Creative Commons; 9 bottom, artem evdokimov/Shutterstock; 9 bottom right, left, djmilic/Shutterstock; 9 bottom right, middle, optimarc/Shutterstock;/Shutterstock; 9 bottom right, right, Dim Dimich/Shutterstock; 10 top, Joel Godwin/Creative Commons; 10 top left, Fab_1/Shutterstock; 10 top right, Chalermphon Srisang/Shutterstock; 10 bottom, Manuel de Corselas/Creative Commons; 11 top, Ato 01/Creative Commons; 11 top right, antoniodiaz/Shutterstock; 11 bottom, Zack Frank/Shutterstock; 11 bottom middle, P. Mullins/Shutterstock; 11 bottom right, Wladyslaw/Creative Commons; 12, Chicago Architectural Photographing Company/Public Domain; 12 right, Public Domain; 13, WiNG/Creative Commons; 13 left, PixelSquid3d/Shutterstock.com; 13 right, sirtravelalot/Shutterstock; 14, LauraKick/Shutterstock;14 top right, Senyuk Mykola/Shutterstock; 14 bottom right, Sonpichit Salangsing/Shutterstock; 15 top, 15 bottom left, j.woottisak/Shutterstock; 15 bottom, James Steidl/Shutterstock; 16 left, S-F/Shutterstock; 16 middle left, InterEdit88/Creative Commons; 16 middle right, Stefan Fussan/Creative Commons; 16 right, Marco Rubino/Shutterstock; 17 top, James Kerwin/Creative Commons; 17 top left, iofoto/Shutterstock; 17 top right, Roman Samborskyi/Shutterstock; 17 middle, Armand du Plessis/Creative Commons; 17 bottom right, Ken Schulze/Shutterstock; 18 top, ArtEvent ET/Shutterstock.com; 18 bottom, Egor Zhuravlev/Creative Commons; 18 bottom left, BearFotos/Shutterstock; 18 bottom right, Valdis Skudre/Shutterstock.com; 19 top, Lucy Li/Creative Commons; 19 top left, Dragon Images/Shutterstock; 19 middle left, Niederkasseler/Creative Commons; 19 middle right, Dllu/Creative Commons; 19 bottom, Anton Galakhov/Creative Commons;/Creative Commons; 19 bottom left, Paul Michael Hughes/Shutterstock; 20 top, Matthew Van Dyke/Shutterstock; 20 middle, Public Domain; 20 bottom, Sergey-73/Shutterstock; 20 bottom left middle, Henning Schlottmann/Creative Commons; 20 bottom left, Design Projects/Shutterstock; 20 bottom right, Silfeb/Creative Commons; 21 top, Barry haynes/Creative Commons; 21 top left, Nanette Dreyer/Shutterstock; 21 middle left, song songroov/Creative Commons; 21 middle right, Carlos Adampol Galindo/Creative Commons; 21 bottom, p_jirawat/Shutterstock.com; 21 bottom right, Chalermphon Srisang/Shutterstock; 22 top, Holger.Ellgaard/Creative Commons; 22 bottom, 22 bottom right, 23 bottom left, 25 bottom left, LightField Studios/Shutterstock; 23 top, USAF/Public Domain; 23 top left, VGstockstudio/Shutterstock; 23 top right, 26 bottom left, Prostock-studio/Shutterstock; 23 bottom, Marcin Kadziolka/Shutterstock.com; 23 bottom middle, CGN089/Shutterstock; 23 bottom right, Jihan Nafiaa Zahri/Shutterstock; 24 top, calado/Shutterstock; 24 top left, Andrey_Popov/Shutterstock; 24 top right, Inside Creative House/Shutterstock; 24 bottom, Patrick Herzberg/Shutterstock; 25 top, alexandre zveiger/Shutterstock; 25 top left, fizkes/Shutterstock; 25 top right, fizkes/Shutterstock; 25 bottom, Ivan Kurmyshov/Shutterstock; 25 bottom right, Happy Together/Shutterstock; 26 top, guruXOX/Shutterstock; 26 bottom, Gorodenkoff/Shutterstock; 27 top, Viltvart/Shutterstock.com; 27 top left, Jeka/Shutterstock; 27 top right, DavideAngelini/Shutterstock; 27 middle, Ezume Images/Shutterstock; 27 bottom, 3000ad/Shutterstock; 28 top left, Stefan Fussan/Creative Commons; 28 bottom left, Wpcpey/Creative Commons; 28–29, Austen Photography

Bearport Publishing Company Product Development Team
President: Jen Jenson; Director of Product Development: Spencer Brinker; Senior Editor: Allison Juda; Editor: Charly Haley; Associate Editor: Naomi Reich; Senior Designer: Colin O'Dea; Associate Designer: Elena Klinkner; Product Development Assistant: Anita Stasson

Produced for Bearport Publishing by BlueAppleWorks Inc.
Managing Editor for BlueAppleWorks: Melissa McClellan
Art Director: T.J. Choleva
Photo Research: Jane Reid

Library of Congress Cataloging-in-Publication Data is available at www.loc.gov or upon request from the publisher.

ISBN: 979-8-88509-165-7 (hardcover)
ISBN: 979-8-88509-172-5 (paperback)
ISBN: 979-8-88509-179-4 (ebook)

Copyright © 2023 Bearport Publishing Company. All rights reserved. No part of this publication may be reproduced in whole or in part, stored in any retrieval system, or transmitted in any form or by any means, electronic, mechanical, photocopying, recording, or otherwise, without written permission from the publisher.

For more information, write to Bearport Publishing, 5357 Penn Avenue South, Minneapolis, MN 55419.
Printed in the United States of America.

Contents

Build It! 4
Amazing Ancient Architecture 6
Cool Castles and Cathedrals 8
Spectacular Symmetry 10
Birth of the Skyscraper 12
How Did They Build That? 14
The World's Tallest 16
Engineering Art 18
Wild, Wacky Buildings 20
Safety First! 22
Going Green 24
Building for the Future 26

Skyscraper Model 28
Glossary 30
Read More 31
Learn More Online 31
Index 32
About the Author 32

Build It!

The next time you're on your way to school, count how many different kinds of buildings you see. There might be houses, apartment buildings, restaurants, or stores. You may even see a barn, a factory, or a sports stadium. Throughout history, people have constructed all kinds of buildings. Today, **engineers** still use building methods from the past. But they've also found new ways to make some pretty extreme structures. Let's get building!

For thousands of years, **shelters** have protected people from weather, animals, and other dangers.

WHOA, YOUR SHELTER LOOKS NICE!

YEAH! AND IT'S GREAT FOR KEEPING THE WILD ANIMALS OUT!

The Citadel of Aleppo in Syria may be one of the world's oldest castles. It was built 5,000 years ago.

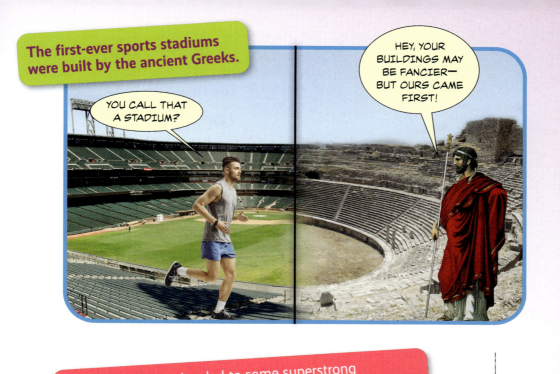

The first-ever sports stadiums were built by the ancient Greeks.

YOU CALL THAT A STADIUM?

HEY, YOUR BUILDINGS MAY BE FANCIER—BUT OURS CAME FIRST!

Smart engineering has led to some superstrong buildings! **Torre Latinoamericana in Mexico City, Mexico, is the tallest building to survive an earthquake.**

Today, most buildings start out the same way. An **architect** designs the structure. Then, engineers plan and oversee the construction.

ALL RIGHT, EVERYBODY. LET'S GET STARTED . . .

Amazing Ancient Architecture

Building impressive structures is nothing new—people from ancient times were expert engineers! The Mesopotamians built amazing **temples** called ziggurats. The ancient Egyptians created their famous pyramids. Ancient Chinese people made an incredible palace complex with nearly 10,000 rooms. And that's not all! Let's look back at the long history of building buildings . . .

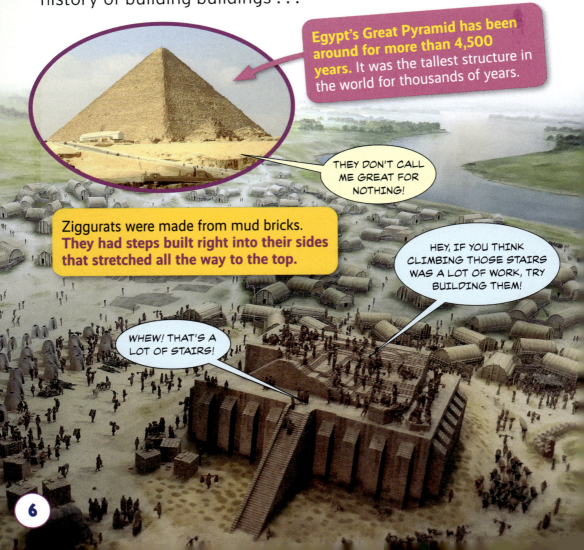

Egypt's Great Pyramid has been around for more than 4,500 years. It was the tallest structure in the world for thousands of years.

THEY DON'T CALL ME GREAT FOR NOTHING!

Ziggurats were made from mud bricks. They had steps built right into their sides that stretched all the way to the top.

HEY, IF YOU THINK CLIMBING THOSE STAIRS WAS A LOT OF WORK, TRY BUILDING THEM!

WHEW! THAT'S A LOT OF STAIRS!

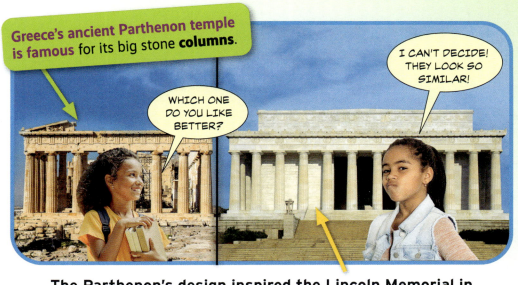

The Parthenon's design inspired the Lincoln Memorial in Washington, D.C.

Cool Castles and Cathedrals

No look at history's most incredible buildings would be complete without a tour of some of the world's coolest castles and **cathedrals**. In **medieval** times, castles were homes for kings and other wealthy people. High, strong walls kept out enemies, and tall towers offered views of the surrounding land. Huge, beautiful stone cathedrals were also built during this time. Many of these grand castles and cathedrals still stand today.

Some castles were surrounded by watery **moats**. Drawbridges over **the moats could be lifted to stop enemies from entering the castles.**

NICE TRY, GUYS!

HEY, NO FAIR!

A castle's thick stone walls kept the people inside them safe.

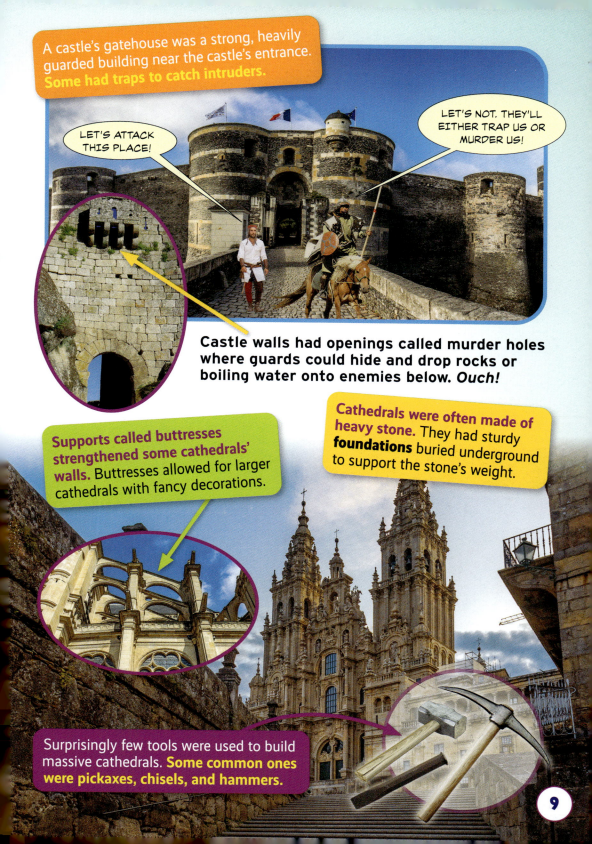

Spectacular Symmetry

Old castles, cathedrals, temples, and pyramids all had something in common—symmetry. Symmetry is when two halves of something mirror one another. Many things in nature are symmetrical, such as leaves and butterflies. The people who built huge structures long ago used symmetry to copy nature's beauty. Oh, and it also helped to make sure buildings were balanced so they wouldn't topple! Many modern buildings have symmetry, too. Let's see what this looks like.

India's Taj Mahal, built in the 1600s, is one of the most famous examples of building symmetry.

More than 1,000 elephants helped move the stone used to construct the Taj Mahal.

Mexico's El Castillo pyramid has four symmetrical sides.

Birth of the Skyscraper

Have you ever looked up at a skyscraper and wondered how such an incredible thing was built? It takes a lot of engineering skill to build these super-tall structures. The first skyscrapers were made in the second half of the 1800s. The use of lighter steel **frames** instead of heavier iron ones made it possible to build taller and taller buildings. Today, skyscrapers soar to amazing heights!

Before these extremely tall buildings existed, **the word *skyscraper* referred to a ship's triangular sail.**

HEY! THANK YOU FOR THE ELEVATOR!

Elisha Graves Otis invented the passenger elevator in 1853. People no longer had to walk up stairs, so buildings could be built taller!

YOU'RE WELCOME!

Chicago's Home Insurance Company Building, finished in 1885, was considered the first skyscraper. It was 10 **stories** tall.

How Did They Build That?

Constructing a skyscraper is similar to making other buildings, just on a much larger scale. A skyscraper needs a strong foundation called a substructure. A deep pit is dug into the ground. Then, strong columns, usually made of steel and concrete, are set into even deeper holes in the pit. From there, the skyscraper can be built up, up, up . . .

Gravity pulls down on a building. A skyscraper must have a strong skeleton of steel beams—called the superstructure—to support its weight.

Steel rods covered in concrete make a strong main structure.

THAT STRUCTURE LOOKS SUPER!

Engineers make sure a **skyscraper's superstructure** can withstand strong winds and earthquakes.

The columns in a skyscraper's foundation are wider at the bottom so they can hold up the building's heavy weight.

Huge cranes lift heavy building materials up the the sky-scraping top.

The World's Tallest

All skyscrapers are amazing feats of engineering, but some are so tall they're in a league of their own! The world's tallest building—at an astounding 2,720 ft (830 m)—is Burj Khalifa in Dubai, United Arab Emirates. Merdeka 118 in Kuala Lumpur, Malaysia, comes in second. Completed in 2021, Merdeka 118 knocked China's Shanghai Tower into third place. Let's take a tour of these and other jaw-dropping skyscrapers . . .

Burj Khalifa, Merdeka 118, and Shanghai Tower are called megatall skyscrapers. **A building is megatall only if it's higher than 1,970 ft (600 m).**

If you laid all the steel bars used in Burj Khalifa's construction end to end, **they'd stretch a quarter of the way around Earth.**

BEING MEGATALL IS THE BEST!

Burj Khalifa is about twice as tall as the Empire State Building.

OH, COME ON! I THOUGHT I WAS TALL!

Burj Khalifa   Merdeka 118   Shanghai Tower   Empire State Building

A bridge connecting the Petronas Towers in Kuala Lumpur is 560 ft (170 m) above the ground. That's a long way down!

THAT BRIDGE IS SO HIGH UP!

YEAH, I GUESS THEY WANTED A SHORTCUT TO THE NEXT BUILDING.

A huge gold-colored ball inside Taiwan's Taipei 101 skyscraper controls swaying during earthquakes to prevent damage to the building.

YEP, THIS IS EXACTLY WHAT WE HAD IN MIND!

New York City's One World Trade Center tops out at 1,776 ft (541 m) tall, in honor of the year the United States declared its independence—1776!

Engineering Art

While some buildings impress us with their sheer height, others are amazing because of their supercool, unique designs. These structures prove that engineers can build foundations, steel, and cement into artsy masterpieces. From a tall, twisted tower to a crooked little house, engineers have found ways to construct buildings that are true works of art!

Flame-shaped buildings in Azerbaijan are covered in screens that show images of flickering flames at night.

The Turning Torso building has a top floor that's turned 90 degrees from the bottom floor. That's a fun spin on engineering!

The Shard is a 95-story building that looks like a jagged piece of glass.

♪ LET'S DO THE TWIST! ♫

The Ray and Maria Stata Center has sharp angles and twisting towers that make it look like it's been crinkled up. *Whoa!*

WOW! WHAT'S UP WITH THAT BUILDING?

Poland's Little Crooked House looks like **a house from a strange fairy tale.**

Check out the **building complex that looks** like a glittering glass castle in Pittsburgh, Pennsylvania.

The 1,516-ft (462-m) tall Lakhta Center in Saint Petersburg, Russia, **looks like a giant spike sticking into the sky.**

OKAY, I SEE YOUR POINT.

19

Wild, Wacky Buildings

Some buildings are considered works of art, while others are famous for being a bit . . . odd. In Pennsylvania, there's a house that looks like a huge shoe. Ohio has a building that looks like a giant basket. There are structures inspired by foods, animals, and even flying saucers. What would your zany building look like if you let your engineering imagination run wild?

In 1948, shoe salesman Mahlon Haines built **the Haines Shoe House out of wire and cement!**

THIS IS A SHOE-IN FOR BEST BUILDING EVER!

Futuro houses, built in the 1960s and 1970s, **were made to look like flying saucers and to be easily moved anywhere.**

Another building compared to flying saucers is the Niterói Contemporary Art Museum in Brazil. Its circular shape is out of this world!

HEY, DON'T THOSE BUILDINGS BELONG TO US?

20

The Big Basket building was used as headquarters for the Longaberger Company. Is it any surprise the company made baskets?

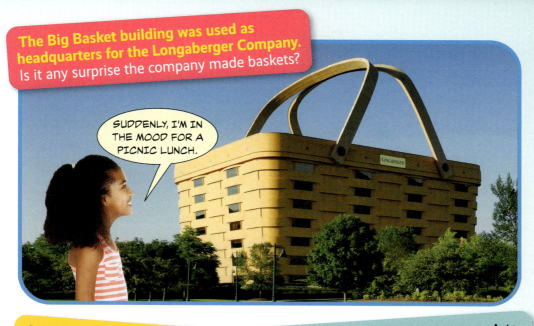

SUDDENLY, I'M IN THE MOOD FOR A PICNIC LUNCH.

A hotel in Huzhou, China, is nicknamed the horseshoe. Can you guess why?

The National Center for the Performing Arts in Beijing, China, **is shaped like a giant egg.**

The Elephant Building in Thailand looks like—that's right—a huge elephant! It's as tall as 33 real elephants stacked on top of one another.

WELL, SHUCKS... I'M FLATTERED!

Safety First!

While those wacky buildings are fun, other buildings have been made for more serious purposes. They're among the safest, most secure places on Earth. Military buildings around the world are designed to defend against attacks. And they aren't the only buildings that are super secure. These strong structures use expert engineering to guard people and valuables. Check them out . . . if you can get past security!

Some high-security buildings are constructed underground! Bahnhof Underground Data Center keeps information stored in a bomb shelter 100 ft (30 m) below a mountain in Sweden.

Fort Knox is where the United States keeps much of its gold. But the shiny stuff is behind a 22-ton (20-t) door for safekeeping!

The doors within Cheyenne Mountain Complex each weigh 25 tn. (23 t).

Going Green

While some structures are made to protect people or things, green buildings are engineered to protect Earth! Green buildings may be constructed with local or recycled materials. They are also sometimes powered by **renewable** energy sources, such as sunlight and wind. This is much better for the planet than burning **fossil fuels**. It's time to go green!

Solar panels on some buildings turn sunlight into energy that powers lights and other things inside.

Some buildings are designed to collect rainwater, which can be used for many things—like flushing the toilet!

Building for the Future

Buildings have changed over time, making our world look much different than it did hundreds of years ago. And there are many more buildings to come. Cities are getting bigger as Earth's **population** grows. It's up to engineers to build better buildings that give people the space they need to live and work. What will these buildings look like?

Large-scale 3D printers are being used more and more to create parts for building construction. This cuts down on waste and helps the planet!

Some engineers and architects are using **virtual reality** to see a building's design before construction begins. Cool!

ARE YOU REALLY DESIGNING A BUILDING? ALL I SEE IS A TABLE.

GET THE VIRTUAL REALITY HEADSET. THEN YOU'LL SEE WHAT I SEE!

Soon, there may be more zero-energy buildings. These buildings produce all their own renewable energy.

LOOK AT ALL THOSE SOLAR PANELS.

YEAH, THEY'RE REALLY ENERGIZED!

Someday, buildings may be repaired by **bacteria**! A special bacteria that grows in water could be used to patch cracks in concrete.

LET'S GO, GUYS! IT'S TIME TO FIX SOME CRACKS!

In the future, buildings may have the technology to keep track of their own energy use. This will help them waste less energy.

MY SENSORS TELL ME YOU'RE WASTING ENERGY!

ME? NEVER! I'M PRETTY SURE YOUR SENSORS ARE WRONG.

Skyscraper Model

Craft Project

Imagine you're an engineer who has to build a skyscraper stretching thousands of feet into the sky. How would you do it? You'd have to start with a strong foundation so the building could stand upright. Then, you'd build it up, taller and taller. This project will let you build your very own skyscraper—the sky's the limit!

Skyscrapers need fast elevators. The Shanghai Tower's elevator travels at nearly 46 miles per hour (74 kph)!

What You Will Need

- Construction paper
- Scissors
- Tape

Hong Kong is the city with the most skyscrapers in the world.

Step One

Cut construction paper into many long, rectangular strips of the same size. Then, cut the same number of squares, making their sides slightly longer than the short side of the strips. These will be supports for your building.

Step Two

Take a strip and fold it in half so its short ends meet. Fold it in half once more the same direction. Unfold and repeat with the other strips.

Step Three

Using the fold lines from Step Two as your guides, fold each strip into a square and tape the ends together. These are the stories of the building.

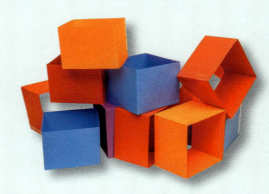

Step Four

Cut a large piece of construction paper for the base. Place the first story in the center of the base. Add a support on top of the story. Repeat, alternating stories and supports. Use tape to stick all the pieces together as you build up your structure. How high can you go?

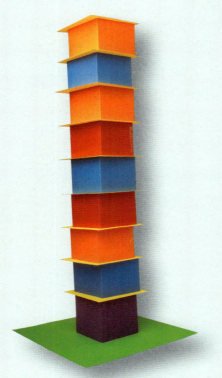

architect a person who designs buildings

bacteria tiny life forms that can be seen only under a microscope

carbon dioxide a gas that is released when fossil fuels are burned

cast iron a metal made from a mix of carbon and iron

cathedrals large churches

columns upright structures that look like poles and are used to support buildings

concrete a hard material made from sand, gravel, cement, and water

data information

engineers people who use science and math concepts to design things, such as buildings, bridges, and roads

fossil fuels energy sources formed from the ancient remains of plants and animals

foundations stone or concrete structures at the bottoms of buildings

frames structures that support larger objects and are made of parts joined together

gravity the force that pulls objects toward Earth's center

medieval related to a period of European history from 500 CE to 1500 CE

moats deep ditches dug around castles and usually filled with water

population the number of people who live somewhere

renewable able to be restored or replaced

shelters structures that protect people or things from weather or danger

stories levels or floors of a building

temples religious buildings where people worship

virtual reality a fake space made by computers that resembles the physical world in sight and sound

Read More

Banting, Erinn and Heather Kissock. *Empire State Building (Structural Wonders of the World).* New York: AV2 by Weigl, 2020.

Miller, Derek. *The STEM of Skyscrapers (The World of STEM).* New York: Cavendish Square, 2021.

Nagelhout, Ryan. *Gareth's Guide to Building a Skyscraper (Gareth Guides to an Extraordinary Life).* New York: Gareth Stevens Publishing, 2019.

Learn More Online

1. Go to **www.factsurfer.com** or scan the QR code below.

2. Enter "**X-Treme Buildings**" into the search box.

3. Click on the cover of this book to see a list of websites.

31

Index

Burj Khalifa 16
castles 4, 8–10, 19
cathedrals 8–10
columns 7, 14–15
concrete 7, 14, 25, 27
earthquakes 5, 14, 17
Empire State Building 13, 16
foundations 9, 14–15, 18, 28
green buildings 24–25
Home Insurance Company Building 12

Otis, Elisha Graves 12
pyramids 6, 10
Shanghai Tower 16, 28
skyscrapers 12–17, 28–29
solar energy 24, 27
stadiums 4–5, 7
steel 12–14, 16, 18
superstructure 14
symmetry 10–11
temples 6–7, 10

About the Author

Catherine C. Finan is a writer living in northeastern Pennsylvania. Her very favorite skyscraper ever is the Chrysler Building in New York City.